Are you there, Bear?

Ron Maris

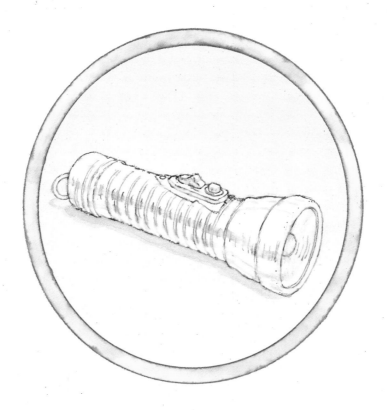

PUFFIN BOOKS

for Ellen Maris

My room is dark and quiet.
Are you there, Bear?

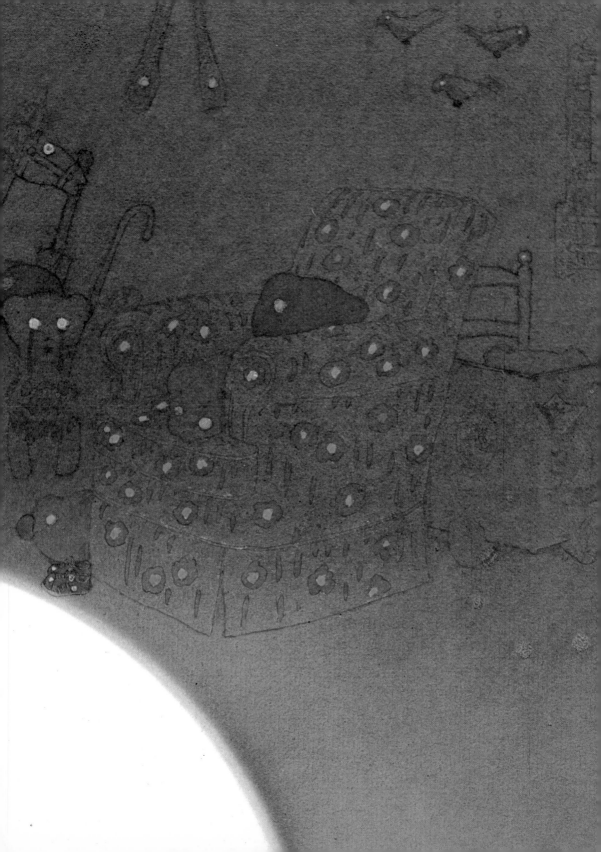

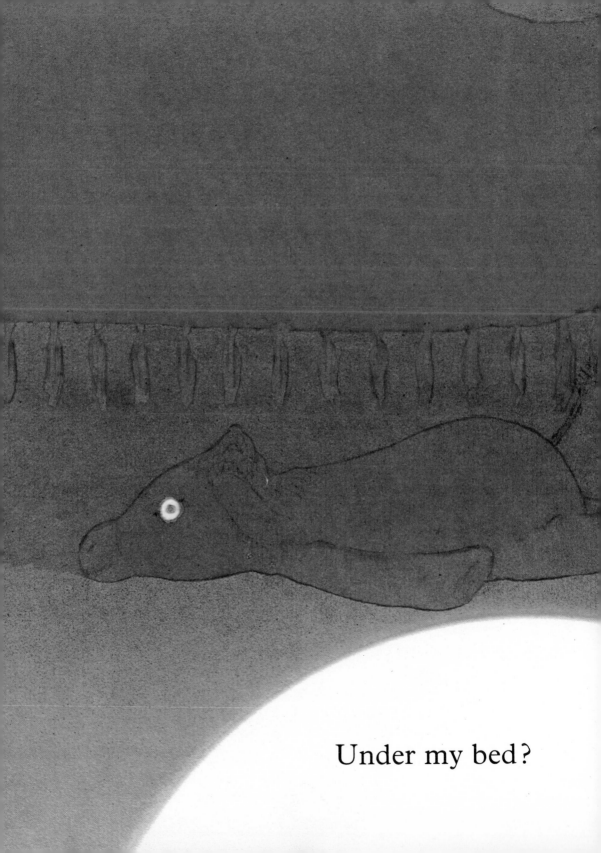

Under my bed?

That's not a bear.
Come out, Donkey!

In my cupboard?

That's not a bear.
Come out,
Little Doll!

Up here, in my box?

That's not a bea
Go back, Jack!

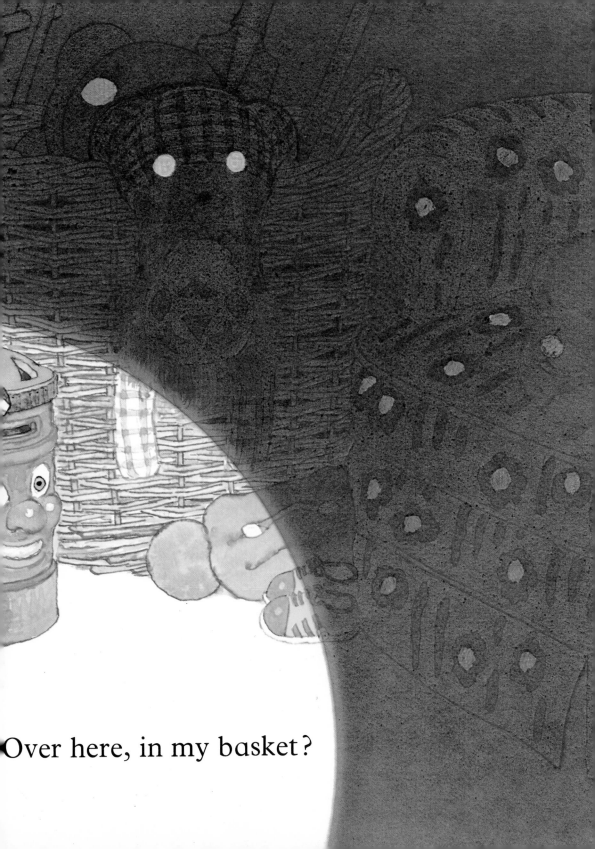

Over here, in my basket?

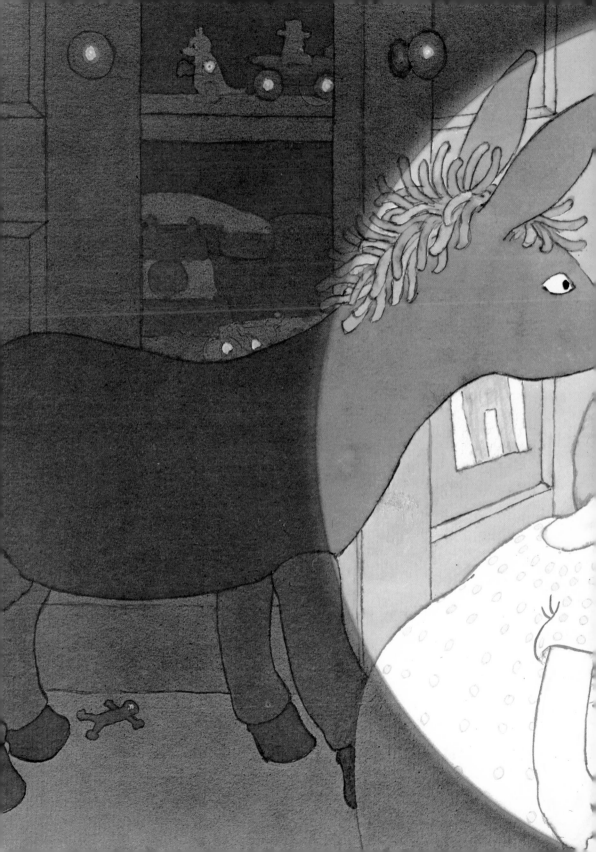

That's not a bear.
Come out, Raggety!

Down there,
on my chair?

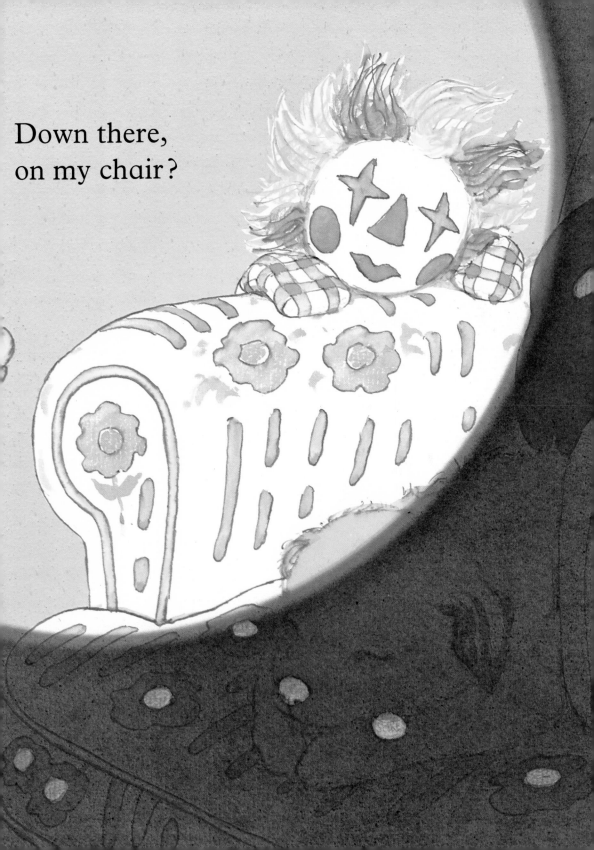

That's not a bear.
Come out, Spike!

What is that?

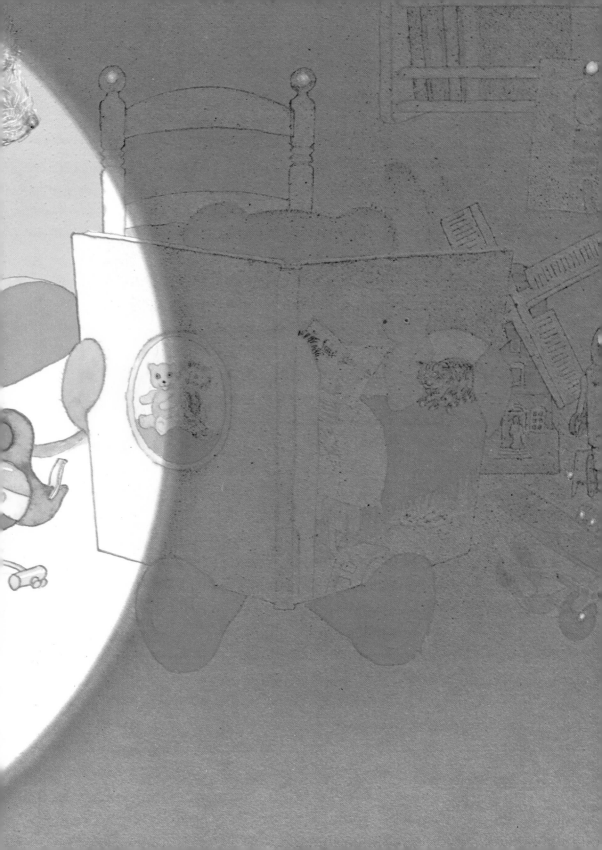

Who is there, beside my chair?

Bear is there! With a book . . .

. . . tell us a story, Bear.